Dear mouse friends,
Welcome to the world of

Geronimo Stilton

THE RODENT'S GAZETTE
EDITORIAL STAFF

Geronimo Stilton
A learned and brainy
mouse; editor of
The Rodent's Gazette

Thea Stilton
Geronimo's sister and
special correspondent at
The Rodent's Gazette

Trap Stilton
An awful joker;
Geronimo's cousin and
owner of the store
Cheap Junk for Less

Benjamin Stilton
A sweet and loving
nine-year-old mouse;
Geronimo's favorite
nephew

Geronimo Stilton

FLIGHT OF THE RED BANDIT

Scholastic Inc.

ISBN 978-0-545-55630-9

www.geronimostilton.com

Published by Scholastic Inc., 557 Broadway, New York, NY 10012. SCHOLASTIC and associated logos are trademarks and/or registered trademarks of Scholastic Inc.

Stilton is the name of a famous English cheese. It is a registered trademark of the Stilton Cheese Makers' Association. For more information, go to www.stiltoncheese.com.

Text by Geronimo Stilton
Original title *Dov'è sparito Falco Rosso?*
Cover by Giuseppe Ferrario (design) and Giulia Zaffaroni (color)
Illustrations by Giuseppe Ferrario (design) and Christian Aliprandi (color)
Graphics by Chiara Cebraro

Special thanks to Tracey West
Translated by Lidia Morson Tramontozzi
Interior design by Kay Petronio

12 11 10 9 8 7 6   15 16 17 18 19/0

Printed in the U.S.A.   40
First printing, January 2014

GRANDSON! GRAAAANDSON!

It was hotter than a SCORCHING bowl of cheese soup that July afternoon. I was in my office at the Rodent's Gazette, trying to start my new BOOK. But I couldn't think of ANYTHING to write about!

Um...

Usually, I like to write about my real-life experiences. Lately, however, nothing at all **INTERESTING** has happened to me. So my mind was as **BLANK** as a slice of mozzarella.

I'm sorry — I just realized that I haven't introduced myself! You may have already guessed who I am. My name is Stilton, *Geronimo Stilton*. I'm the editor of *The Rodent's Gazette*, the most **FAMOUSE** newspaper on Mouse Island.

Anyway, I haven't had an adventure in a long time. I thought about my trip to Japan with Wild Willie.* And the time I **SAVED** a beached white whale on a faraway shore.**

Those were great adventures!

Then it hit me. Both of those adventures took place in nature!

Suddenly, I had an **IDEA**: I could write

---

* Read all about it in my book *The Way of the Samurai.*
** Read all about it in my book *Save the White Whale!*

Tweet!

Tweet!

about nature! But what kind of nature? Sandy beaches? LEAFY jungles? PEACEFUL forests?

I LOOKED outside the window and sighed. Holed up in my office in New Mouse City, the only nature I could see were the **sparrows** that pecked at my cheese crusts on the windowsill. They were cute, but I didn't think they would make a very interesting book.

I needed something **exciting** to write about. And to do that, I needed to go on a really good adventure! (But nothing too dangerous, because I am really a SCAREDY-MOUSE at heart!)

I was lost in my thoughts when I heard a

loud **bang**! A mouse pushed open my office door. Can you guess who it was?

I'll give you some clues: He's a tall, muscled mouse with thick silvery **fur**. He wears steel-framed eyeglasses, and he always has a **STERN** look on his face — a very stern look. Now can you guess?

I Find My Inspiration!

You guessed it! That rodent was none other than my grandfather William Shortpaws, also known as Cheap Mouse Willie.

"**Graaaaandson!**" his voice boomed out. It looked like he was in a bad mood, as always.

Graaaaandson!

I noticed that he was wearing his favorite **Hat**: a vintage **cowboy** hat. A red bandanna was wrapped around it, and a falcon's feather was stuck in it.

My grandfather loves hats almost as much as he

loves cheese. He has a big collection of hats, but he wears his **cowboy** hat all the time.

Grandfather took off his hat and showed me a HOLE in the top.

"Know why this hole is here?" he asked. "Because I've been wearing this hat for thirty years. Know something else? I need a **new** one. Want to know one more thing? I need **someone** to go get it for me."

I knew that he meant me, of course, but I didn't have time to go hat shopping.

"Excuse me, Grandfather," I said **POLiteLy**. "But I have a book to write, and I need to find some inspiration."

"I'll give you some inspiration!" he **THUNDERED**.

"You will?" I asked nervously.

"That's right!" Grandfather replied. "I bought my hat years ago in a *little shop*

Grandfather William Shortpaws's Hat Collection

Cowboy Hat
Style: Silver Cactus Deluxe
Made in: Sedona, Arizona, USA

in Sedona, Arizona. It was called the Silver Cactus. And this red bandanna was given to me by my friend the **RED BANDIT** many years ago. He wears one just like this."

"Arizona?" I asked. I had never been there.

"Oh, it's a marvelous state, and Sedona is so **beautiful**!" my grandfather said. "That's why you will find it the perfect setting for your next adventure! You'll find lots of **excitement** there."

"What makes it so *exciting*?" I asked cautiously.

"Why, the poisonous snakes, of course!" Grandfather answered. "And then there are all those spiders."

I turned **pale**.

"Yes, some of those **SPIDERS** are as large as a cheese pizza," Grandfather went on. "And don't forget the **scorpions**.

Those little guys are just loaded with poison."

"S-snakes? S-spiders? S-scorpions?" I shuddered.

Grandfather tugged on one of my whiskers. **"SNAP OUT OF IT!"** he yelled. "Are you a scaredy-mouse?"

"N-no, sir," I said.

"We'll see about that," Grandfather said. "You want to call yourself a **REAL MOUSE**?

Then prove it. See if you can go to Arizona and come back in one piece. I am sending your cousin Trap with you to keep an **EYE** on you."

A real mouse?

"Trap!" I exclaimed. I'd almost rather go on a trip with a scorpion.

. . . or a scaredy-mouse?

Grandfather ignored me. "You will go to Sedona, Arizona, and look for the **Silver Cactus** shop," he went on. "There you can buy me another hat just like this one. To get the bandanna and the feather, you'll have to look up my good friend the **RED BANDIT**."

This trip was sounding **WORSE** and **WORSE**. "But I don't know anything about Arizona!" I protested.

Grandfather shoved a guidebook into my

paws. "Then read this!"

Before I could argue, he pushed me out of my office, down the stairs, and shoved me into a *taxi*.

"Take my grandson to the airport, and do it PRONTO!" he barked at the driver.

"But I haven't packed!" I yelled.

Grandfather jammed his **hat** onto my head. "This is all you need."

Then he shut the door with a *bang* that shook my whiskers.

Remember my tiny gift!

"Go find the hat!" he said. "Be sure it's the **RIGHT** size, the **RIGHT** style, and the **RIGHT** color. And don't forget the bandanna and the feaaaaaather!"

As the taxi sped off, I heard his last request.

"By the way, would you take the Red Bandit a †iNY ℊ⸵FT from me?" he yelled. "Trap has it!"

I stuck my head out of the window, and my whiskers waved in the breeze.

"I wiiiiiill, Grandfather!" I shouted back.

You Call That a Tiny Gift?

We got to the airport in a half hour. As soon as I walked in, I heard someone shout, "**GERONIMO!** Stop daydreaming about **cheese sandwiches** and get over here!"

It was my cousin Trap! I've known him ever since we were teeny-tiny mouselets. When we were growing up, Trap loved to play **tricks** on me and **tease** me. And guess what? He still does!

Hee, hee!

All done!

TRAP'S TRICKS, PRANKS, AND JOKES

"Geronimo, get the cheese out of your ears and listen up!" Trap told me. "I need to tell you three important things! *Three!*"

THING NUMBER ONE: Because YOU are always daydreaming, Grandfather wants ME to keep an eye on you in Arizona.

THING NUMBER TWO: Grandfather wants me to make sure that you take good care of a tiny gift for his friend the Red Bandit.

THING NUMBER THREE: Did you know that hat you're wearing makes you look ridiculous?"

Then he turned and pointed to something behind him.

"Here is the tiny gift for Grandfather's friend," he said.

I couldn't believe my eyes. The "tiny gift" was an enormouse jar of **chocolate** cheese spread! It was as high as a mouse, as wide as a barrel, and it looked as heavy as **A BABY ELEPHANT**.

"You call that a †îNᚣ ᚷîᖴ†?" I cried. "Holey cheese! How are we going to lug this all the way to Arizona? What if it breaks?"

Trap shrugged. "That's your problem, Cousin," he said. "Grandfather told **YOU** to bring the enormouse jar and asked **ME** to keep an eye on you. So if the enormouse jar breaks, it'll be **YOUR** fault. You'll have to tell Grandfather . . . and if that happens, I wouldn't want to be in your ᖴᚢᖇ, I'll tell you that!"

Then Trap winked at me. "Know what else? I've got a real **YEN** to know what it tastes like."

Before I could stop him, he shimmied up the side of the enormouse jar. Then he **popped** open the lid. The wonderful smells of **chocolate** and cheese filled the airport.

"Trap, no!" I yelled. "Grandfather will be really *cheesed off*!"

Trap ignored me. He gazed down into the jar. "You've got to see this!" he called down to me. "It looks *super delicious*!"

"Trap, get down!" I yelled again.

"But it's amazing," Trap said. "All the different chocolaty cheesy *flavors* are *swirled* together. No wonder it's called *Chocolate Cheese Delight*!"

"Yeah, sounds great," I said. "Now get down!"

But Trap wasn't even listening to me. His eyes **gleamed**. He hungrily licked his lips.

"**YUM YUM YUM!**" he said. "I've got to have a taste before I flip my whiskers!"

Then he stood on the edge of the jar, like he was *going to dive in. . . .*

CHOCOLATE CHEESE DELIGHT

THIRTEEN FLAVORS!

Chocolate and cheese flavors swirled together:

1. Milk chocolate
2. Cheddar cheese chocolate
3. Hazelnut chocolate
4. Swiss cheese chocolate
5. Very dark chocolate
6. Gorgonzola cheese chocolate
7. White chocolate
8. Mozzarella cheese chocolate
9. Spicy chocolate
10. Cream cheese chocolate
11. Raisin chocolate
12. Stinky cheese chocolate
13. Cherry chocolate

CHOCOLATE CHEESE DELIGHT

THREE FEARS AND
THREE SURPRISES

I grabbed Trap by the tail and **PULLED** him down just in time! I could not let Trap ruin the †ïNY ℊïℱ† for the Red Bandit. If I wasn't watching carefully, he could gobble up all of the tasty **CʜocoLate Cʜeese DeLiᵍʜt!** To be safe, I bought a **LOCK** for the enormouse lid of the enormouse jar.

As we checked in our luggage (including the **enormouse** jar), we heard an announcement.

"The flight to **Arizona** is now boarding at Gate Three."

And so the **LºNGEST** trip ever started. We began by flying all the way from New Mouse City and across the United States to the city of Phoenix, Arizona. Trap **snored** the whole way there. It sounded like a ***train engine*** in my ear!

Me? I stared out the window, *worrying* about three things.

FEAR NUMBER ONE:

Would Arizona be dangerous?

FEAR NUMBER TWO:

Would I be able to keep the enormouse jar from breaking before I delivered it to the Red Bandit?

FEAR NUMBER THREE:

Would I even be able to find the Red Bandit?

I couldn't stop thinking about the **RED BANDIT**. He sounded like a bad guy in a cowboy movie. How had he and Grandfather become **friends**? I wished that I knew more about him. All I knew was to start my search in **SEDONA**, Arizona.

I read through the guidebook. Sedona sounded like a **nice** little town. I especially liked the sound of the "mild climate" the book said it had. *Maybe it*

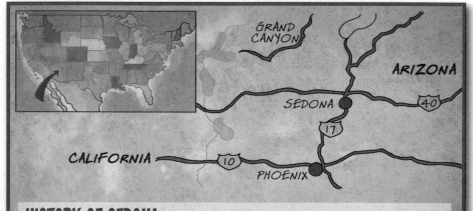

HISTORY OF SEDONA: The city of Sedona lies in the Verdant Valley of Arizona. The valley's early inhabitants mostly hunted and gathered for their food. In 1876, the first nonnative settler claimed property there, and others followed. One settler, Theodore Carlton Schnebly, established a post office there in 1902 and named it — and the town — after his wife, Sedona.

won't be too hard to find the Red Bandit, I thought.

Finally, the plane landed in **PHOENIX**. We rented a **TRUCK** so we could take the two-hour drive to Sedona. But of course, Trap forgot to put gas in it — so we had to stop in the middle of nowhere!

Trap and I had to **hike** the rest of the

We ran out of gas!

way. Guess who had to carry the enormouse jar!

When we got to Sedona, I had **three** surprises.

SURPRISE NUMBER ONE: Sedona wasn't a tiny settlement anymore. It had grown into a lively city of more than 10,000 inhabitants! How would I ever find the Red Bandit?

SURPRISE NUMBER TWO: In July, Sedona's "mild climate" felt more like an oven's temperature!

SURPRISE NUMBER THREE: The enormouse jar of Chocolate Cheese Delight strapped to my back was about to boil over!

I had to find a way to keep the jar **safe** — or face Grandfather's wrath.

I tried to SHADE the enormouse jar with a HUGE patio umbrella.

Wow, it's heavy!

CHOCOLATE CHEESE DELIGHT

ENTERING

SEDONA

ELEVATION   4

FOUNDED   1

AN ARIZONA MAIN STREET

SEDONA: Sedona is located in the heart of Arizona, and is about 115 miles north of Phoenix. It is one of the biggest tourist attractions in the state, thanks to its natural beauty. It has a mild climate, lots of sunshine, and is home to sandstone formations known as red rocks. Visitors to Sedona enjoy outdoor activities such as hiking, biking, golf, tennis, horseback riding, and excursions in helicopters or hot-air balloons.

Then I tried to **cool** it down by fanning it, but that didn't work. So I got lots and lots of **ice cubes** and put them on the lid.

It was no use! The spread was starting to **melt**! Trap began to lick his whiskers in anticipation.

"Cuz, we should eat this **chocolate** now. *RIGHT NOW!* Want me to get some bread to **spread** it on?" Trap asked. **"NO!"**

"Crackers?"

"NO!"

"Cookies?"

"NO!"

"Okay," Trap said. "So we'll just **dive** in then, right?"

"No!" I **YELLED**, getting **angry** now. **"NO, NO, NOOOOOOOO!** I have to give this spread to the Red Bandit or Grandfather will have my WHiSKeRS!"

Luckily for me, Trap gave in. We headed out to find the **Silver Cactus** shop that Grandfather had told me about.

NICE HOWL, CUZ!

In the center of Sedona, there are lots of shops selling everything from outdoor gear to Native American art. Finally, we noticed a **curious-looking** shop tucked away in a **DARK** alley in the oldest part of the city. . . .

Scorpion on the mat! **+** Coyote howl doorbell!

The doormat had a picture of a scorpion that looked so real, I **JUMPED** back with a loud *"Squeak!"* **1** Then I rang the bell and heard the loud howl of a coyote: "АААААА○○○○○○○○○○!" **2**

At the counter, I heard the sound of a rattlesnake. . . . rattle . . . rattle . . . rattle . . . **3** I shrieked again, terrified, and Trap chuckled. "Nice howl, Cuz!" **4**

Yikes!

3

Rattle . . .

+ Fake rattlesnake!

Ha, ha, ha!

Squeak!

4

= Boy, did I feel silly!

Trap took notes on the store's clever pranks. Once I stopped shivering from fright, I showed Grandfather's hat to the shopkeeper. The young rodent shook his head.

Sob!

"We haven't made that style of hat in years," he said. "I'm sorry."

My whiskers **drooped** with disappointment.

"Well, do you know the **RED BANDIT**?" I asked.

He shook his head again. "Sorry, never heard of him."

Now my ears drooped with disappointment. I was headed for the exit when I heard a loud voice from the rear of the shop.

"Hey you! Did you say '**RED BANDIT**'?"

I gazed into the shadows and saw a **BIG**

HISTORY OF THE SILVER CACTUS:
This shop has been in the Ratthide family for more than 150 years. During the gold rush it supplied hats to the daring pioneers who came out West to find their fortune.

CHOCO
CHE
DELIC

GRAY rodent with a thick mustache. He wore a **hat** that looked a bit like my grandfather's. He got up off his chair and walked toward me.

"My name's Tom. **Tom Ratthide**," he said, shaking my paw **vigorously**. "Just hearing the Red Bandit's name reminds me of old times . . . riding across the **desert** with him and my friend William Shortpaws."

"Williams Shortpaws is my grandfather!" I exclaimed in **SURPRISE**. "He sent me all the way here to buy him a new hat."

Tom **ripped** the hat off my head and looked at the label.

"Hmm," he said, stroking his **mustache**. "I remember this style. We sold the **DELUXE Silver Cactus** at least thirty years ago!"

He began to **RUMMAGE** through an old trunk. "They don't make hats like that anymore," he said. Then he grinned. "Aha! Found it!"

He held up a hat that looked exactly the same as my grandfather's. It had the same **Silver Cactus** charm dangling from the band. Only the falcon feather and RED bandanna were missing. I hoped that the

Here it is!

RED BANDIT could give me those — if I could ever find him.

Tom tucked the hat into a hatbox. I tried to pay him, but he refused.

"Take it to your grandfather William as a token of our old, undying **FRIENDSHIP**," he said. "As for the Red Bandit, start your search at **Cathedral Rock**. That's where I saw him last."

Then he looked me **UP** and **DOWN**. He handed me a card with the words **WILD RAT ADVENTURES** on it. "Better talk to these rodents. You're going to need some help out there in the **desert**."

I thanked him and left the shop, **EAGER** to continue. I was one step closer to the Red Bandit. . . .

Mr. Skilton, You're Really Silly!

When I left the shop, I found Trap **YAWNING** on a park bench.

"Cuz, while you check out that adventure place, I'll stay here and **meditate** on the situation," he said. "And don't forget to take the **ENORMOUSE JAR**. I wouldn't want anyone to take it while I'm fast aslee — I mean, while I'm meditating!"

Wake up!

Zzzzz

Trap **spread** out and was **snoring** in three seconds flat! I tried to **shake** him awake, but my cell phone **rang**. It was my **sister**,

Hi, Ger!

Thea. I asked her to join me in Arizona. She's a great rodent to have around when you're in a **JAM**.

"Sorry, Ger," she replied. "You'll have to do the best you can without me. I'm working on a **pretty strange** new story and I can't get away."

"I understand," I said with a sigh.

"Oh, I almost **FORGOT**," she added. "Grandfather Shortpaws says to *HURRY* up and find the Red Bandit. And don't you dare break that **ENORMOUSE JAR**!"

I glared at the **ANNOYING** jar. "I'll do my best."

With another sigh, I strapped the enormouse jar onto my back and headed to **WILD RAT ADVENTURES**. When I stepped inside the office, an **athletic**-looking mouse with a long black braid approached me. She looked me up and down, just like Tom Ratthide had.

I sucked in my **belly** — I haven't gone to the gym lately, but I have made many trips to my refrigerator! I knew she had me pegged: a city mouse with **pitiful** muscles, wearing the **WRONG** clothes for hiking and carrying an **ENORMOUSE JAR** of chocolate on my back.

She unrolled a brochure that was ten feet long. "Poppy Spritely, at your service," she said. "Here at Wild Rat Adventures we provide **GUIDED** adventures of every type. What would you like to do? *Extreme* hang gliding? *Extreme* hiking? *Extreme* camping?"

I **clumsily** tried to bow, but the enormouse jar threw me off-balance, and I fell **FLAT** on my face in front of her.

"Pleased to meet you," I said. "My name is Stilton, Geronimo Stilton!"

She picked me up, *chuckling.* "I'm pleased to meet you, too. You look like a giant turtle!"

Holey cheese! I was **EXTREMELY** embarrassed. But I guess I did look like a **giant**

turtle with that enormouse jar on my back.

She looked me over again. "You know, I'm not certain if you're the type of mouse who can handle our *extreme* tours. I'm sorry."

I **frowned**. Poppy Spritely was probably right, but I didn't know how else I would get to Cathedral Rock.

"That's too bad," I said. "Tom Ratthide said you could **HELP** me."

She smiled. "That changes everything!" she exclaimed. "Normally, I'd send a city mouse like you right out of here. You are

not the type for *extreme* adventures, trust me. But if you insist, I'll see if I can find something that's not too extreme, Mr. Skilton."

"The name is Stilton. S-T-I-L-T-O-N," I corrected her. "And I need you to take me to Cathedral Rock as soon as possible. I'm in a **HURRY**!"

Her eyes got **wide**. "You? To Cathedral Rock? **Impossible!**"

"But I must," I insisted.

She shook her head. "Mr. Spilton, you

Be careful!

CHOCOLATE CHEESE LIGHT

Argh!

won't be able to **hack it**. I know what I'm talking about."

Now, if she had read any of my **books**, she might have known that I am no stranger to *extreme* adventures. But clearly, she hadn't, so I had to convince her.

"My name is Stilton with a *t . . . t* for *tenacious*," I said. Then I fell to my knees. "Pleeease? It's an *emergency*. If I don't find the Red Bandit and get that **FALCON FEATHER** and bandanna, my grandfather will have my whiskers!"

"You should have told me that you were looking for a **red falcon**," she said, clearly confused. "You must be an **ORNITHOLOGIST**. Probably a famouse bird scientist. In that case, I can help you. In fact, I have the **PERFECT** guide for you!"

"**NO**, I'm looking for the Red *Bandit*, and

he might have a falcon *feather*," I tried to explain, but Poppy wasn't listening.

She ran around the office, grabbing a map, a backpack, a rope, a compass, and other **emergency** supplies. Then she grabbed me by the paw and **DRAGGED** me out the door.

"*HURRY UP!*" she urged. "Time flies, and the falcons won't wait for us!"

And that's how we began . . . *five extreme adventures!*

EXTREME ADVENTURE #1

We left the office and picked up Trap, who YAWNED and stretched.

"We can go now," he said. "I've meditated enough for one day."

Poppy tied the enormouse jar to the roof of her ALL-TERRAIN VEHICLE. We piled in and she drove down a bumpy dirt road.

"Don't worry, Mr. Svilton!" she said. "You are in good PAWS with Wild Rat Adventures."

I wanted to interrupt and tell her that my name is *Stilton*, with a *t*, but she was talking too *FAST*.

"I will find your red falcon, or my name isn't Poppy Spritely!" she boasted. "But if you ask me, Mr. Smilton, we should drop this enormouse jar. It will slow us down!"

Maybe the heat was getting to me, but I kind of FREAKED out.

"My name is *STILTON*! With a *t*!" I yelled. "And I **CANNOT** get rid of that enormouse jar or my grandfather will have my whiskers!"

Trap winked at her. "Don't pay any attention to him, Miss Spritely," he said. "He's just a little excited."

POOR ME! I didn't even have Trap on my side. Fortunately, they both stopped BUGGING me because we had arrived at the foot of Cathedral Rock!

CATHEDRAL ROCK: Cathedral Rock is one of the most impressive of the red rock formations in Sedona. A steep trail leads hikers almost a mile up the side of the rock.

"Get your **paws** ready, gentlemice," Poppy said as she got out of the vehicle. "The **BEST** is yet to come!"

Trap and I got out and I strapped the enormouse jar to my back. I looked up at the tall rocks silhouetted against the **sky**. Just the thought of climbing to the top made me feel as **clammy** as cold cheese sauce.

"Excuse me, Miss Spritely, but do we really need to go all the way to the top?" I asked. "I'm not sure I can make it."

She slapped me on the back so hard that I almost **TOPPLED** over.

"Don't worry, Shilton," she said. "If you don't make it, I'll arrange a nice little **FUNERAL** for you. Feel better now?"

That did *not* make me feel better, but I had no choice. I took a deep breath and followed Poppy and Trap up the steep trail.

Trap WHISTLED as he climbed, light as a FEATHER. And Poppy Spritely scurried up the trail very quickly and well . . . spritely, just like her name!

I slowly plodded along. The enormouse jar felt HEAVIER and HEAVIER with each step.

I COULDN'T keep up, and soon I lost sight of both of

Faster!

Puff . . . puff!

them. Once in a while, I would hear Poppy call from the top of the trail.

"*HURRY UP*, Skilton! Soon it will be **night**, and we won't be able to find the falcons."

Poppy still thought we were looking for **BIRDS**, but I had my eyes peeled for the Red Bandit.

Then Poppy **scrambled** down the trail, handing me her binoculars.

"**LOOK, SPILTON!**" she commanded. "I found a red falcon."

Red
Falcon

Red
Bandit

I sighed. "Poppy, I keep trying to tell you, I am not looking for a **RED FALCON**, I'm looking for —"

"Just look!" she said impatiently, thrusting the binoculars in front of my eyes.

Through the lenses I saw an **ANNOYED**-looking red falcon in her nest. I was about to **complain** to Poppy again when I noticed something far, far in the background.

EXCITED, I focused the lenses. In the distance, I saw an elderly rodent riding a horse. The rodent wore a hat that looked just like my grandfather's!

"Holey cheese!" I cried. "It's the **RED BANDIT**!"

I had finally found my grandfather's friend!

EXTREME ADVENTURE #1, PART 2

"We've got to get to the valley, **FAST**!" I shouted. "The Red Bandit is down there!"

Spritely **ripped** the binoculars out of my paws. "Smilton, you're so *silly*!" she said. "Why didn't you tell me you were looking for the Red Bandit?"

I couldn't believe my ears. "But I . . ."

"The only way to get to that valley is to **CLIMB**," she said. Then she started pulling **EQUIPMENT** out of her pack and attaching it to me: microfiber pants and a shirt, a helmet, a harness, a belt with hooks, and a rope.

"But I'm *not* a professional climber!" I protested. I'm a professional SCAREDY-MOUSE!

"Don't worry, you'll be **fine** — I think,"

Poppy said. "You look like a **STRONG** mouse (sort of), and I'll hold on to the rope up here — if I can! Just take nice long **BOUNCES** down the rocks!"

"**BOUNCES?**" I asked. That didn't sound very safe. "And what about the enormouse jar of chocolate cheese spread?"

Poppy strapped the enormouse jar to my back.

"Hopefully, it'll **BREAK** on the way down," Poppy said. "And don't worry about

Helmet

Microfiber suit

Climbing harness

Hooks

your grandfather having your WHiSKeRS. You won't have any whiskers to worry about if you don't get down the mountain **SAFELY**."

I looked over the **edge** of the cliff. I took a deep breath, getting ready, when suddenly . . .

"**GO!**" Poppy yelled. Then she pushed me off the side of the cliff!

"**HEEEEEELP!**" I screamed.

"Remember to bounce, Spilton!" Poppy called out. "I'll see you back in Sedona!"

I bounced down the side of the mountain, **gripping** the rope tightly in my paws. With every hop, I was sure the enormouse jar would crush me.

It was truly an extreme adventure!

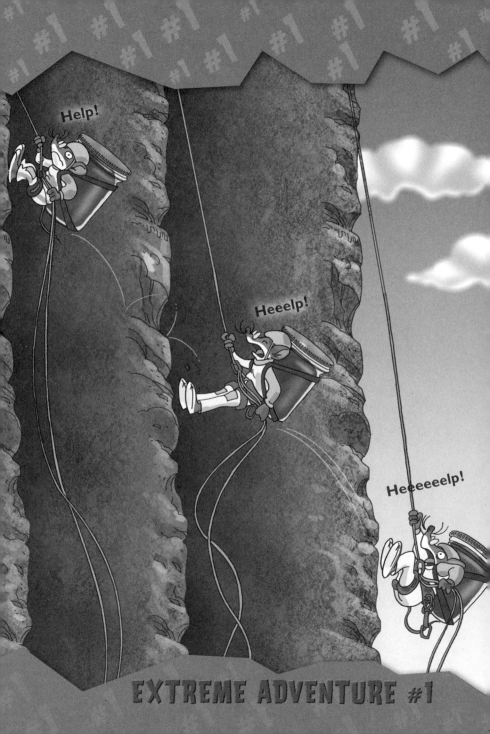

EXTREME ADVENTURE #2

The enormouse jar and I made it to the BOTTOM of the mountain in one piece. As soon as my paws touched the GROUND, I passed out from fright!

Then I felt cold water splashing my face. I opened my eyes and saw a rodent standing over me.

"Are you all right, Greenhorn?" he asked in a booming voice.

Then I recognized him. It was Wild Willie!

"This is lightning," he said, pointing to a black horse. "If you want to catch up to the Red Bandit, hop on the saddle!

Wild Willie
The most daring mouse on Mouse Island!

But be careful! He's the **wildest** horse in Arizona."

Before I could protest, he forced me to put on a cowboy outfit: a ***fringed*** shirt, **LEATHER** pants, and boots with ***spurs***. Then he put me on the horse.

"But I don't know how to ride!" I yelled.

He **snorted**. "Don't worry, you'll learn! Thea sent me to help you. Are you ready for an ***extreme*** adventure?"

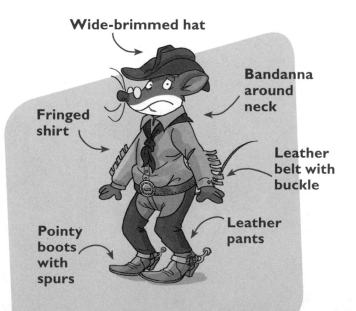

Wide-brimmed hat

Bandanna around neck

Fringed shirt

Leather belt with buckle

Pointy boots with spurs

Leather pants

I was about to answer that I was definitely *not* ready for that when my cell phone **rang**. It was my sister, Thea.

"Geronimo, did you find the Red Bandit?" she squeaked anxiously. "Grandfather is worried! And don't break the enormouse jar."

"Everything's fine so far, Thea, but Wild Willie wants me to *ride* — whoa!"

Lightning suddenly took off like . . .

LIGHTNING! I didn't have time to say good-bye to Wild Willie. I **pulled** on the reins, but the horse didn't stop.

"Heeeelp!" I screamed, **TERRIFIED**.

Lightning galloped down a narrow path, **ZIGZAGGED** toward the **RIGHT**, zoomed to the **LEFT**, and then raced up and down a line of little hills. Then he decided to show off by bucking and rearing, **rodeo style**, and I tumbled off his back!

EXTREME ADVENTURE #3

I **crashed** into the ground like a meteorite! Then I bounced up and into a patch of **thorny** cactus plants. **OUCH!** My poor little behind was covered in *sharp* spikes! **1**

I bet you think that things couldn't get any worse, right? **WRONG!** I **LEAPED** out

Aargh!

CHOCOLATE

Ugh!

1 I landed on a cactus. . . .

2 I fell in a pile of puma poo. . . .

of the cactus patch . . . and landed in a pile of puma poo! **2** Yuck! With a disgusted SHRIEK, I sprang to the **right** — and stepped on a rattlesnake's tail! **3**

I *darted* to the left, but this time I trampled a scorpion! **4**

I JUMPED away from the scorpion . . . and landed on a tarantula! **5** With a scream, I ran away and found the **ENORMOUSE JAR** (which had luckily landed on some

Oops!

Holey cheese!

3 I stepped on a snake's tail. . . .

4 I trampled a scorpion. . . .

cacti and didn't break). 6 Then I scampered down the path as fast as I could. 7

The sun had already set, so I **RAN** . . . and **RAN** . . . and **RAN**. But there was no sign of the Red Bandit anywhere.

Holey cheese, where am I? I wondered.

Then I realized that I was back near downtown Sedona. The first stars were

Boing!

Whew!

CHOCOLATE DELIGHT

5 I landed on a tarantula. . . .   6 I found the enormouse jar. . .

beginning to play peekaboo in the clear **BLUE** night sky. The **Arizona** sky was amazing. As tired as I was, its beauty really TOUCHED my heart.

Hop! Hop!

Ooooh!

I scampered the entire night.

EXTREME ADVENTURE #4

I parked myself in front of the door of the adventure agency and promptly fell asleep on the doormat. I woke up when Poppy opened the office.

"Tsk, tsk, Skilton," she said. "Haven't you found the **RED BANDIT**?"

Then her cell phone *rang*, and she answered. "Hello? **WHAT?** You spotted the Red Bandit? **WHERE?** At the bottom of the Grand Canyon? **WOW!** We're on our way right now!"

She **DRAGGED** me inside the office and outfitted me with a pair of khaki pants, a khaki shirt, hiking boots, and a cap with a visor to prevent the sun from  **TOASTING** me like grilled cheese. Then she lathered my fur with 150 SPF **SUNSCREEN** lotion.

She drove us to a hotel, where we picked up Trap, and then we headed for the **GRAND CANYON!** (Of course, we took the enormouse jar with us.)

Trap looked happy and refreshed that morning. He wouldn't stop talking about how **comfortable** the hotel was.

"I spent the night in an *elegant* four-star hotel," Trap bragged. "I met a lovely mouse, and we dined on a **delicious** cheese soufflé in the LUXURY restaurant. Later, a group of FUN rodents and I went for a midnight swim under the stars. I slept like a king in a VeRY SOft bed. When I woke up, I took a BATH in a tub with massaging jets. Just as my tummy was starting to rumble, room service delivered

a mouth-watering cheese omelet right to my door. What about you, Cuz?"

I showed him my tail, which was still full of cactus SPIKES.

"I **rappelled** down a **mountain** . . . got thrown off a horse . . . was **Pricked** by cactus spikes . . . stepped in puma poo . . . narrowly missed a rattlesnake, a scorpion, and a tarantula . . . **blistered** my paws walking across the desert . . . slept on a doormat . . . and skipped breakfast!"

As I was talking, the vehicle came to a stop at the edge of a **STEEP** cliff! I bit down on my tongue. **OUCH!**

My poor tongue swelled up. I got out and looked over the edge of the cliff.

"**WHaD itH iD?**" I asked with my swollen tongue.

"Sfilton, this is the Grand Canyon!" Poppy exclaimed. "It is one of the world's greatest natural **wonders**."

"**Beauthiful!**" I exclaimed.

Trap strapped the enormouse jar to my pack and **SHOVED** me onto the path that led to the bottom of the canyon. I turned to him, surprised.

"**Thrap, aren'd you coming?**" I asked.

He held up the hatbox. "Nope. I need to stay behind and keep an eye on Grandfather's new hat."

I wanted to **complain**, but Poppy urged me on. "Smilton, hurry up! Your next guide is waiting for you. If you move fast, you just might find the **RED BANDIT**!"

"Id's a **long** way down," I protested.

"Well, you can take the trip by mule if you want," Poppy said. "Unless you want to walk."

My poor paws were still aching from the night before. "I'll dake the **MULE**, pleath! Thad'll be much easier."

Boy, was I **wrong** about that!

Cap with visor

Khaki pants and shirt

Hiking boots

EXTREME ADVENTURE #4, PART 2

A rodent as big as a truck appeared with a mule and plopped me on top of the impatient animal. My guide wore mirrored sunglasses, and it took me a second to recognize him. . . . It was Bruce Hyena!

Bruce Hyena
The most adventurous mouse on Mouse Island!

"Bruce, is that you?" I asked, relieved that my tongue was finally better.

"Hey there, CHEESEHEAD!" Bruce said.

"What are you doing here, Bruce?" I asked.

"I got a summer job

taking **CHEESEHEAD** tourists like you to the bottom of the canyon," he answered.

"How many tourists do you lose per year?" I asked **nervously**.

Bruce just **SNICKERED** and climbed on another mule. He clicked his tongue and the mules started to carry us down the very **NARROW**, very **steep**, and very scary trail. My mule **swayed** back and forth, making my tummy flip-flop.

Then I looked down into the **canyon**. What a **mistake**! My head began to spin. My whiskers started to drip with sweat. Then I suddenly felt **cold** all over, and my teeth started to chatter.

CLACK CLACK CLACK! CLACK CLACK CLACK! CLACK CLACK CLACK! CLACK CLACK CLACK!

Panicked, I grabbed the mule's neck and

THE GRAND CANYON: The Grand Canyon is an immense gorge that is 277 river miles long, 18 miles wide, and 1 mile deep. It was carved by the Colorado River in the northern part of Arizona. It is managed by the Grand Canyon National Park, one of the major national parks in the United States.

hugged it tightly. Then I closed my **EYES** so I couldn't see.

But I couldn't shake the feeling that I was going to **FALL**, so I decided to walk. It wasn't much better. With every step I took, I was sure I would **plummet** into nothingness. *Squeak!*

Bruce laughed at me. "You're impossible, Cheesehead! Get back on your mule — he won't fall, I promise! I'll tie you to him and blindfold you so you don't get **dizzy**! You'll be as cozy as a caterpillar in a cocoon!"

It was no use protesting. Bruce tied me up and used the **RED** bandanna from Grandfather's hat for a blindfold.

Even though I couldn't see, the **SWAYING** of the mule made

Cozy as a caterpillar in a cocoon!

my tummy **FLIP-FLOP** again. My stomach started to gurgle.

Glaaarb! Glooorb! Gluuurb!

Poor me! Besides having carsickness, airsickness, and seasickness, I found out that I also suffer from mule sickness!

It was an extreme adventure for my stomach!

EXTREME ADVENTURE #5

When we FINALLY got to the bottom of the Grand Canyon, Bruce released me from my cocoon. My knees were WOBBLY, and my whiskers were trembling.

Bruce slapped my back with enough force to bring down a buffalo. "Good luck finding the **RED BANDIT**, Cheesehead!" he said. "Just try to stay alive, okay?"

He and the mules headed back up the path. I **LOOKED** around for the Red Bandit, but I didn't see him.

Then I noticed a group of **hikers** who were about to go rafting down the Colorado River.

"Excuse me, but have any of you seen a rodent with silver fur, a **cowboy hat**, and a red bandanna around his neck?" I asked.

"Sure did!" replied an **ATHLETIC**-looking mouse. "We saw him heading for that valley just a little while ago."

"You did?" I asked, **EXCITED**.

She nodded. "Would you like us to give you a ride? We're going that way."

A ride sounded very nice. "**Thank you**," I squeaked gratefully.

She handed me a helmet, a wet suit, and a **life jacket**, and then shoved a paddle in my paw.

I jumped into the raft. Extreme adventure number five was about to begin!

The raft bobbed up and down on the **raging** river while the guide shouted instructions.

"**Paddle** right! **Paddle** left! **Paddle**

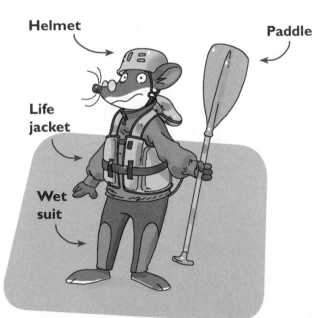

Helmet

Paddle

Life jacket

Wet suit

hard! **Paddle** smoothly! Whatever you do . . . just **paddle**!"

As we traveled, breathtaking beauty unfolded all around me. The high, steep banks of the **red rocks** reflected into the river, and the sky above was a **BRiLLiaNt** shade of blue that can only be found in the desert.

Suddenly, the raft **LURCHED** to the right, and then to the left. We almost tipped over! The other mice shouted with glee.

"**FANtaaaaaastic!**"

"**Awwwwwwesome!**"

Me? I shrieked with **terror**!

The blonde hiker **winked** at me enthusiastically.

"Isn't this incredible?" she shouted over the deafening sound of the roaring waves.

I was thinking that it was an incredibly **extreme adventure** . . . maybe too extreme for a mouse like me. But I didn't tell her that.

Suddenly, the roaring of the waves became **LOUDER** and **LOUDER**. The guide's voice got louder and faster.

"Paddle, paddle, paddle, paddle!" he cried. "And be careful not to fall into the wat —"

Too Late!

I Am the Red Bandit

I **PLUMMETED** into the river, and the weight of the **ENORMOUSE JAR** strapped to my back sent me straight to the bottom like a stone. I'm not sure how I did it, but I managed to swim to the surface.

I *gasped* for air as the strong current tossed me up and down. I sank again and my mouth filled with water. I was sure my lungs would **BURST**!

PAWING with all my might, I reached the surface once more. The swift-moving **CURRENT** took me downriver with incredible speed.

The current **DRAGGED** me close to shore. As I floated under a tree branch extending over

the water, I felt a paw pluck me by the neck and haul me out of the river. A **GENTLE** voice whispered, "Don't give up!"

Then I **fainted**. When I came to, I saw two pairs of dark little eyes, as ripe as berries, staring at me curiously. Then two **shrill** little voices yelled, "Grandpop, he's awake!"

An elderly rodent with **silver fur**, a cowboy hat, and a red bandanna around his neck came closer and **smiled** at me. That's when I recognized him: It was the

same rodent who'd *FISHED* me out of the river, the same one I had seen riding a horse in the valley. . . .

It was the **RED BANDIT**!

His eyes twinkled with **amusement** under the brim of his cowboy hat.

"Welcome to my home, Geronimo," he said.

STUNNED, I opened my eyes wide and said, "How do you know who I am?

Did Grandfather tell you I was coming?"

He shook his head. "Nope! He couldn't have. I don't have a phone or **eLectRicity**."

He took a faded photo from his pocket and showed it to me.

Grandfather William
Aunt Sweetfur
Geronimo
Thea

"Your grandfather sent me this photo years ago," he said. "I recognized you right off. You haven't **changed** much."

I looked around and realized that I was inside a **LOG CABIN** — a house made entirely out of **WOOD**.

I was tucked inside a cozy bed and wrapped in a quilt. The quilt looked handmade out of **colorful** fabric squares. In the room, there was also a nightstand, a rug, a wooden table, a stool, a rocking chair, some

small baskets, and a fireplace brightened by a warm, CRACKLING FIRE.

Through a small window I could see a slice of sky studded with stars. I realized that this house was built with love and inhabited by happy rodents.

The **RED BANDIT** nodded, as if he had heard my thoughts. "Yes, Geronimo, I built this house with my own two paws many years ago. I don't need a lot of stuff in order to be happy. I just want to be in touch with nature, and to protect it the best I can."

I nodded sleepily.

"We'll talk tomorrow, Geronimo," he said. "Have I got some yarns to share with you!"

I wanted to thank him, but I quickly drifted into a deep, deep sleep. I dreamed that Grandfather William was nervously pacing back and forth across my office, waiting for his new hat. . . .

When I woke up, morning **sunlight** streamed through the window. I felt much, much better. The Red Bandit loaned me some **cowboy** clothes. To thank him, I helped out with some chores around the cabin, doing tasks just like they did in the days of old. . . .

THANKS, FRIEND!

I stayed with the Red Bandit and his **GRANDCHILDREN** for several days, until I was feeling better. The Red Bandit took care of me while Cody and Bonnie kept me company. We became such good *friends* that they asked if they could call me *uncle*! That made me so **happy**.

On the third day, Trap, Poppy, Wild Willie, and Bruce Hyena showed up at the cabin. They had formed a *SEARCH PARTY* to find me!

"Good for you, Sbilton!" Poppy exclaimed. "You're still alive!"

Wild Willie slapped my back. "I'm proud of you, **Rookie**," he said.

Bruce chuckled. "Cheesehead! It's good

to see you alive. And you're in **tip-top** shape!"

Trap hugged me. "Cuz, I thought you were a goner for sure this time!"

Then he looked around anxiously. "I have Grandfather's hat safely here in the hatbox, but where's the enormouse jar?" he

Hi, Cuz!

Good job, Rookie!

Cheesehead!

asked. "Do you have it? Did it get **broken** in the river?"

I **smacked** a paw on my forehead. **Cheese niblets!** I had completely forgotten about Grandfather's hat and the

enormouse jar of **CHOCOLATE CHEESE DELIGHT**.

I started to sweat. It must have gotten **smashed** in the river. Grandfather would have my whiskers for sure!

Trap's cell phone *rang*, and he handed it to me. It was Thea.

"Ger, I was worried sick about you!" she said. "Are you all right? Did you find the **RED BANDIT**? And did you deliver the enormouse jar of Chocolate Cheese Delight in one piece?"

I had to tell her the truth . . . sort of. "Well,

I didn't find the Red Bandit. . . . He found me! He **FISHED** me out of the river. As for the jar, tell Grandfather that everything's okay — I hope. I'll give the jar to the Red Bandit right away . . . if I find it . . . so he can open it up . . . if it's not broken to bits."

"Broken to bits?" Thea asked, but **luckily**, the Red Bandit walked in, rolling the **ENORMOUSE JAR**!

"Is this what you're **LOOKING** for, Geronimo?" he asked. "I fished it out of the **river** along with you. I put it in the stable to stay cool."

Thank goodness! The **ENORMOUSE JAR** was safe!

"Red Bandit, this is a gift from my grandfather," I explained. "He said to tell you: 'Here's a gift just as **sweet** and **enormouse** as our friendship.'"

Red Bandit's eyes got wide. "This gift is truly enormouse!"

Cody and Bonnie brought in a ladder and placed it next to the **ENORMOUSE JAR**. The Red Bandit climbed to the top, opened the lid with a *plop*, and dipped a paw into the **chocolaty**, **cheesy** spread. Then he tasted it.

"How is it?" Trap asked eagerly.

The Red Bandit grinned. "**Dee-licious!**" he exclaimed. "Go ahead, have some!"

Everyone grabbed a spoon or a ladle and dipped it into the jar. We put the spread on bread and cookies.

Trap didn't even bother with any bread. He **GOBBLED** the spread down by the ladleful! Nobody minded, though, because the jar was so enormouse that there was **plenty** for everyone.

"This gift is **extremely** awesome, **extremely** special, and **extremely** delicious!" everyone agreed.

When we had all eaten our fill (even Trap), the Red Bandit took off his red bandanna and handed it to me, *smiling*.

"Please give this **bañdañña** to my friend William," he said. "A long time ago, I gave him one just like it."

For William!

Then he pulled the falcon's **FEATHER** from his hat and handed it to me. "An object as special as a falcon's feather cannot be bought. It can only be found or received as a gift. I'm giving this to William as a sign of our friendship."

Filled with **GRATITUDE,** I took the feather from him. I tied the bandanna around Grandfather's new hat and tucked the **feather** into the band. Thanks to the Red Bandit, Grandfather **finally** would have his new hat, complete with the bandanna and falcon's feather. I hadn't failed him. I felt as happy as a rodent in a **cheese factory!**

A New Hat for William Shortpaws

With our tummies filled with excellent **chocolate** and cheese, we said our good-byes. Trap and I got ready to begin our very long journey back to Mouse Island, where my grandfather William waited for us.

I promised to visit my new *friends* again with my entire family. Next time, I would stay a lot longer, because **ARIZONA** is a truly amazing, beautiful, and friendly state.

The plane ride was **very**, **very**, **very** long. I slept almost the entire time — not only was my adventure in Arizona physically exhausting, but it was very *emotional*, too.

When the plane finally **LANDED** I woke with a start. Trap and I picked up our luggage from **BAGGAGE** claim and then

headed toward the *exit*. Who do you think was waiting for us?

It was a very **IMPATIENT** Grandfather William, along with Thea and my nephew Benjamin! Grandfather William ran toward me, shouting, "**Well? Do you have it? Where is it?**"

I handed him the hatbox.

"Here it is, Grandfather," I said. "Here's your hat."

MOVED, he took the hat and put it on his head. "Perfect!" he said with a grin.

"It fits my head **perfectly**, just like the other one."

I pointed to the R E D bandanna and the falcon's feather.

"Your friend the Red Bandit sent these to you as gifts," I said. "I met him after I climbed and rappelled down Cathedral Rock, rode on a wild horse through the desert, took a mule down the Grand Canyon, and rafted down a RAGING RIVER."

Grandfather looked at me in amazement. "YOU climbed Cathedral Rock? YOU rafted down a raging river and did all of those other EXTREMELY DANGEROUS things . . . for me?"

He slapped my back. "Good for you, Grandson!" he said PROUDLY. "You're getting GOOD. Almost as good as me! I

also lived through many FUR-RAISING adventures in Arizona. Ah, those were the good old days."

He looked at the bandanna and feather one more time. "Did the Red Bandit like my Little gift?" he asked anxiously.

"And how!" Trap yelled. "He had us all taste it. That chocolaty cheesy spread was YUMMY, YUMMY, YUMMY!"

I had one more thing for Grandfather. I handed him an envelope. "This letter is for you from the **RED BANDIT**," I said.

He read the letter out loud.

Dear William,

I miss our friendship. Why not come for a visit with your whole family? That way, my family would get to know your family. We'll be waiting for you in the log cabin in the woods!

Sincerely,
The Red Bandit

Grandfather **smacked** his forehead. "Holey cheese! That's a **great** idea!" he exclaimed. Then he turned toward Benjamin and Thea.

"Get ready," he said. "Our next vacation

will be in Sedona, **ARIZONA**! I'm sure we'll have many wonderful adventures there!"

"Just as long as they're not extreme," I muttered. Then everyone cheered.

"Hooray for Grandfather William!"

"*Hooray for Arizona!*"

"**Hooray for the Red Bandit!**"

I hugged Benjamin and whispered in his fuzzy ear.

"You're in for such a **treat**! You'll have lots of fun with Cody and Bonnie," I promised. "But you may also **LEARN** something, my dear nephew."

"What's that, Uncle?" Benjamin asked.

I smiled, remembering my **peaceful** days in the cabin. "In Arizona, I found the key to happiness: a simple life in harmony with nature, surrounded by the people you love."

I give you my word on that, dear readers, or my name isn't *Geronimo Stilton*!

Don't miss any of my other fabumouse adventures!

#1 Lost Treasure of the Emerald Eye

#2 The Curse of the Cheese Pyramid

#3 Cat and Mouse in a Haunted House

#4 I'm Too Fond of My Fur!

#5 Four Mice Deep in the Jungle

#6 Paws Off, Cheddarface!

#7 Red Pizzas for a Blue Count

#8 Attack of the Bandit Cats

#9 A Fabumouse Vacation for Geronimo

#10 All Because of a Cup of Coffee

#11 It's Halloween, You 'Fraidy Mouse!

#12 Merry Christmas, Geronimo!

#13 The Phantom of the Subway

#14 The Temple of the Ruby of Fire

#15 The Mona Mousa Code

#16 A Cheese-Colored Camper

#17 Watch Your Whiskers, Stilton!

#18 Shipwreck on the Pirate Islands

#19 My Name Is Stilton, Geronimo Stilton

#20 Surf's Up, Geronimo!

#21 The Wild, Wild West

#22 The Secret of Cacklefur Castle

A Christmas Tale

#23 Valentine's Day Disaster

#24 Field Trip to Niagara Falls

#25 The Search for Sunken Treasure

#26 The Mummy with No Name

#27 The Christmas Toy Factory

#28 Wedding Crasher

#29 Down and Out Down Under

#30 The Mouse Island Marathon

#31 The Mysterious Cheese Thief

Christmas Catastrophe

#32 Valley of the Giant Skeletons

#33 Geronimo and the Gold Medal Mystery

#34 Geronimo Stilton, Secret Agent

#35 A Very Merry Christmas

#36 Geronimo's Valentine

#37 The Race Across America

#38 A Fabumouse
School Adventure

#39 Singing
Sensation

#40 The Karate
Mouse

#41 Mighty
Mount
Kilimanjaro

#42 The Peculiar
Pumpkin Thief

#43 I'm Not a
Supermouse!

#44 The Giant
Diamond Robbery

#45 Save the
White Whale!

#46 The Haunted
Castle

#47 Run for the
Hills, Geronimo!

#48 The Mystery
in Venice

#49 The Way of
the Samurai

#50 This Hotel Is
Haunted!

#51 The
Enormouse Pearl
Heist

#52 Mouse in
Space!

#53 Rumble in
the Jungle

#54 Get into
Gear, Stilton!

#55 The Golden
Statue Plot

#56 Flight of the
Red Bandit

The Hunt for the
Golden Book

Don't miss these exciting Thea Sisters adventures!

Thea Stilton and the Dragon's Code

Thea Stilton and the Mountain of Fire

Thea Stilton and the Ghost of the Shipwreck

Thea Stilton and the Secret City

Thea Stilton and the Mystery in Paris

Thea Stilton and the Cherry Blossom Adventure

Thea Stilton and the Star Castaways

Thea Stilton: Big Trouble in the Big Apple

Thea Stilton and the Ice Treasure

Thea Stilton and the Secret of the Old Castle

Thea Stilton and the Blue Scarab Hunt

Thea Stilton and the Prince's Emerald

Thea Stilton and the Mystery on the Orient Express

Thea Stilton and the Dancing Shadows

Thea Stilton and the Legend of the Fire Flowers

Thea Stilton and the Spanish Dance Mission

Thea Stilton and the Journey to the Lion's Den

Thea Stilton and the Great Tulip Heist

Be sure to read
all of our magical
special edition
adventures!

THE KINGDOM OF FANTASY

THE QUEST FOR PARADISE:
THE RETURN TO THE KINGDOM OF FANTASY

THE AMAZING VOYAGE:
THE THIRD ADVENTURE IN THE KINGDOM OF FANTASY

THE DRAGON PROPHECY:
THE FOURTH ADVENTURE IN THE KINGDOM OF FANTASY

THE VOLCANO OF FIRE:
THE FIFTH ADVENTURE IN THE KINGDOM OF FANTASY

THEA STILTON: THE JOURNEY TO ATLANTIS

THEA STILTON: THE SECRET OF THE FAIRIES

Join me and my friends on a journey through time in this very special edition!

THE JOURNEY
THROUGH TIME

Meet
CREEPELLA VON CACKLEFUR

I, *Geronimo Stilton*, have a lot of mouse friends, but none as **spooky** as my friend CREEPELLA VON CACKLEFUR! She is an enchanting and MYSTERIOUS mouse with a pet bat named Bitewing. YIKES! I'm a real 'fraidy mouse, but even I think CREEPELLA and her family are AWFULLY fascinating. I can't wait for you to read all about CREEPELLA in these fa-mouse-ly funny and **spectacularly spooky** tales!

#1 The Thirteen Ghosts

#2 Meet Me in Horrorwood

#3 Ghost Pirate Treasure

#4 Return of the Vampire

#5 Fright Night

Meet
GERONIMO STILTONOOT

He is a cavemouse — Geronimo Stilton's ancient ancestor! He runs the stone newspaper in the prehistoric village of Old Mouse City. From dealing with dinosaurs to dodging meteorites, his life in the Stone Age is full of adventure!

#1 The Stone of Fire

#2 Watch Your Tail!

#3 Help, I'm in Hot Lava!

#4 The Fast and the Frozen

ABOUT THE AUTHOR

 Born in New Mouse City, Mouse Island, **GERONIMO STILTON** is Rattus Emeritus of Mousomorphic Literature and of Neo-Ratonic Comparative Philosophy. For the past twenty years, he has been running *The Rodent's Gazette*, New Mouse City's most widely read daily newspaper.

Stilton was awarded the Ratitzer Prize for his scoops on *The Curse of the Cheese Pyramid* and *The Search for Sunken Treasure*. He has also received the Andersen 2000 Prize for Personality of the Year. One of his bestsellers won the 2002 eBook Award for world's best ratlings' electronic book. His works have been published all over the globe.

In his spare time, Mr. Stilton collects antique cheese rinds and plays golf. But what he most enjoys is telling stories to his nephew Benjamin.

1. Main entrance
2. Printing presses (where the books and newspaper are printed)
3. Accounts department
4. Editorial room (where the editors, illustrators, and designers work)
5. Geronimo Stilton's office
6. Helicopter landing pad

THE RODENT'S GAZETTE

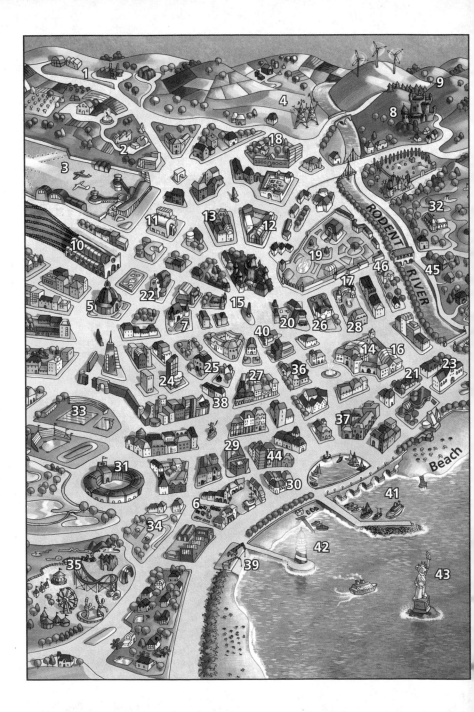

Map of New Mouse City

1. Industrial Zone
2. Cheese Factories
3. Angorat International Airport
4. WRAT Radio and Television Station
5. Cheese Market
6. Fish Market
7. Town Hall
8. Snotnose Castle
9. The Seven Hills of Mouse Island
10. Mouse Central Station
11. Trade Center
12. Movie Theater
13. Gym
14. Catnegie Hall
15. Singing Stone Plaza
16. The Gouda Theater
17. Grand Hotel
18. Mouse General Hospital
19. Botanical Gardens
20. Cheap Junk for Less (Trap's store)
21. Aunt Sweetfur and Benjamin's House
22. Mouseum of Modern Art
23. University and Library
24. *The Daily Rat*
25. *The Rodent's Gazette*
26. Trap's House
27. Fashion District
28. The Mouse House Restaurant
29. Environmental Protection Center
30. Harbor Office
31. Mousidon Square Garden
32. Golf Course
33. Swimming Pool
34. Tennis Courts
35. Curlyfur Island Amusement Park
36. Geronimo's House
37. Historic District
38. Public Library
39. Shipyard
40. Thea's House
41. New Mouse Harbor
42. Luna Lighthouse
43. The Statue of Liberty
44. Hercule Poirat's Office
45. Petunia Pretty Paws's House
46. Grandfather William's House

Brigand's Isle

This way to the Rodent Straits

Tomcat Island

Pirate Ship of Cats

2 3 4

1

Cat's Claw Bay

Panther Archipelago

Hamster Islands

Blue Dolphin Bay

6 7

5

Swissville

Coral Reefs

25

8

14

This way to the Mousific Ocean

9

Stray Cat Harbor

32

San Mouscisco

10

12

11

13

Cheddarton

23 Mouseport

This way to the Ratlantic Ocean

15

21

20

22

26

17 16

29 19

New Mouse City

18

35

24

30

Mousefort Beach

28

27

31 36

33

34 37

Furflung Island

N
W   E
S

This way to the Sea of Mice

MOUSE ISLAND

Map of Mouse Island

Dear mouse friends,
Thanks for reading, and farewell
till the next book.
It'll be another whisker-licking-good
adventure, and that's a promise!

Geronimo Stilton